CW00644456

Taffy Thomas trained as a literature and drama teacher at Dudley College of Education and taught for several years in Wolverhampton before founding and directing the legendary folk theatre company, Magic Lantern, and the rural community arts company, Charivari, with their popular touring unit, the Fabulous Salami Brothers. He performed all over Europe until, at the age of 35, he suffered a stroke. Taffy turned back to storytelling as self-imposed speech therapy, and now has a repertoire of hundreds of stories, tales and elaborate lies, collected mainly from traditional oral sources. He has appeared at the National Storytelling Festival in the USA and the Bergen International Festival in Norway and, in 2001, performed a new collaboration for the Blue Peter Prom at the Royal Albert Hall. He is currently Artistic Director of Tales in Trust at The Storyteller's Garden in Grasmere, in the Lake District. In the 2001 New Year Honours List, he was awarded the MBE for services to storytelling and charity. He tours nationally and internationally, working in both entertainment and education, and is also a patron of the Society for Storytelling. In January 2010 he became the UK's first Laureate for Storytelling, which was a two-year honorary post, and in 2013 he was selected as Outstanding Male Storyteller in the British Awards for Storytelling Excellence.

To Alexander Matthew and Joshua

TAFFY'S COAT TALES

A collection of stories from
Taffy Thomas, MBE
Laureate for Storytelling 2010-2012

Love + Legends

Taffy MBE

Tales In Trust

Taffy's Coat Tales

Published by Tales in Trust, 2015

Tales in Trust
The Storyteller's House
Oak Bank
Rydal Road
Ambleside
Cumbria
LA22 9BA

www.taffythomas.co.uk

First published in Great Britain by
The Literacy Club, January 2010

Copyright © Taffy Thomas, 2010

The right of Taffy Thomas to be identified as the author of this work has been asserted by him in accordance with the Copyright, Designs and Patents Act, 1988.

This book is sold subject to the condition that it shall not, by way of trade or otherwise, be lent, resold, hired out, or otherwise circulated without the publisher's prior consent in any form of binding or cover other than that in which it is published and without a similar condition including this condition being imposed on the subsequent purchaser.

All rights reserved. Apart from any use permitted under UK copyright law, no part of this publication may be reproduced, stored in a retrieval system, or transmitted, in any form or by any means without prior written permission by the publisher.
For permission to reproduce extracts in whole or in part, please contact the above publisher at the postal address shown on this page.

All work is reproduced by kind permission of the author. All work is assumed to have been produced by the author, and free of copyright, and The Literacy Club LLP accepts no responsibility for any infringement on behalf of the author, whether intentional or otherwise.

A CIP catalogue record for this book is available from The British Library
ISBN 978-0-9541068-2-9

This book has been typeset in Trebuchet MS and Charlemagne Std
Printed and bound in Great Britain by Xpedient Print Services, Swansea, Wales
www.xpedientprint.co.uk
Cover: Photograph © Steve Barber Photography

DEDICATION

This collection is dedicated to the people who keep alive the storytelling tradition, past, present and future; especially those who have never thought of themselves as storytellers, or called themselves storytellers.

The author would like to thank:

The late Duncan Williamson, mentor, inspiration and source of many of the tales in this collection.
My many other sources – all of which are acknowledged in the provenance that proceeds each tale.
Editor, Helen Watts.
Birmingham Poet Laureate, Adrian Johnson, and the 'guardians of the story', Brian Patten, Michael Rosen, Simon Thirsk, Del Reid, Patsy Heap and Peter Chand, who invited me to be the first National Laureate for Storytelling.
Paddy Killer, simply the finest textile artist in Europe for accepting the commission of the Tale Coat, the National Lottery and Northern Arts for funding the Tale Coat project.
Ryan Walker, for clerical and photographic assistance. All other photos are thanks to Steve Barber, Pieter Koster and Louise Hemsley.
Chrissy Thomas, wife, muse and fierce critic, for keeping the faith!
Yourselves, for buying the book.
Now get telling the stories to help fulfil my brief as National Laureate for Storytelling.

Enjoy!

CONTENTS

Foreword by Mike O'Connor   9
Introduction – 'The story of the Tale Coat'   11
Author's note   15

• The king's own storyteller   17
• A woman's burden   23
• The tiger and the four antelope   25
• Davey and the fish   29
• Singing to the moon   35
• The Stanhope fairies   37
• The clever wish   42
• The legend of the devil's bridge   44
• The cat fishers   49
• The sea morgan   54
• Inna and the eel   57
• King of the birds   62
• Sedna, princess of the sea   66
• The coney   71
• Coyote and the fire witch   74
• The king's tailor   77
• The cobblestone maker   82
• The hunchback and the swan   85
• Coat Tails   89

The Storyteller's Garden   92
The nation's first Laureate for Storytelling   94
Other publications by Taffy Thomas MBE   96

FOREWORD

by Mike O'Connor

The master storyteller travelled the length and breadth of the country. People would come from miles around to hear him tell his tales. He was so famous that someone had made him a special storytelling chair from which he delivered his words of wisdom; and the chair was so grand that some thought it was a throne. He was so famous that someone else had made him a Tale Coat. This was not a piece of smart formal wear, but a lovely coat on which were embroidered scenes from his stories.

One day, he was telling stories to some children. In turn they came forward and studied the Tale Coat, found interesting pictures, and asked for the story to be told. All day they were spellbound by the wonderful tales.

Eventually, there was just one little girl left. She had been late arriving, so she was the last to choose. She studied the Tale Coat carefully, but then burst into tears.

"What's the matter?" asked the storyteller.

"All the stories have been chosen," she said. "It's because I was late. There is no picture left for me – just an empty space."

"Why were you late?" asked the storyteller in a kindly way.

"I fell asleep," said the little girl, "And when I was asleep I had the most amazing dream."

"What was it about?" he asked.

"It was very confusing," she said. "It was about the old days and about the future. It was about here and it was about far-away places. It was about love and hate, war and peace, youth and age, life and death. It was about all those things, but somehow I don't really know what it was about."

Then the master storyteller reached behind his famous chair and took from his bag a small paper waistcoat and some crayons, which he gave to the girl.

"Take these," he said. "On the waistcoat draw the story of today. But leave lots of space. For I can tell, you too are a storyteller, and in time your jacket will have many stories shown upon it. But take care how you draw, for, as you have proved today with my Tale Coat, there must always be room for one more.

THE STORY OF
THE TALE COAT

THE IDEA

For almost 30 years, Taffy Thomas the storyteller had been taking his art to the public at large: as a street theatre performer and puppeteer with his company Magic Lantern (England's unique travelling show), and as the leading storyteller in the North, performing in pubs, schools, at festivals and on his 'Stop Me and Hear One' tricycle.

Then, one day, while walking along Grafton Street in Dublin, Taffy came across a street poet displaying a list of a hundred or so poems, which he could recite to order: if you paid your pound you borrowed a cane and pointed to your choice. Taffy was inspired. Would it be possible to carry with him a lucky dip sack of story ideas so that audience members could determine a choice of tale, as they would select a favourite piece of music from a jukebox? It could be the perfect way to pass control to the audience, allowing them to choose the next story. Their participation would create the show.

Soon after, Taffy was invited to a wedding, for which the male guests were asked to wear top hats and tailcoats. Taffy hit upon the idea of inventing the Tale Coat – a coat with images linked to his stories, echoing the time when, early in his career, he had worn a white lab coat and invited his listeners to paint an image from his stories upon it. Donning the Tale Coat would turn Taffy into a story jukebox.

THE CREATION OF THE TALE COAT AND PORK PIE HAT

Having conceived the idea of the Tale Coat, Taffy needed to find an artist who could create a piece of art he was prepared to wear and use every working day.

While he was Storyteller in Residence at the National Garden Festival in Gateshead, 1990, he would regularly park his 'Stop Me And Hear One' tricycle at the Craft House. It was there that he first saw the work of Paddy Killer, a Yorkshire craftsperson, and for some time a resident on Tyneside. Taffy enjoyed looking at Paddy's counterpanes, wall hangings and hats, noting that she liked to use words and lettering within her work. She, in turn, liked to ask the storyteller for a tale whenever time allowed. A couple of years later, when funding became available for the creation of the Tale Coat, thanks to the Northern Arts and the Arts Council of Great Britain through the National Lottery, it was Paddy Killer who was commissioned to make the piece.

Paddy was asked to base her design for the Tale Coat on a traditional gentleman's smoking jacket and hat. Other than that, she was allowed complete artistic freedom. Knowing that Taffy occasionally tells porky-pies, Paddy delved into her grandmother's cookery book, *Mrs Beeton's Book of Household Management*, borrowing heavily from the illustration of the hand-raised pork pie in designing the hat.

After warning the storyteller that he must not put on weight,

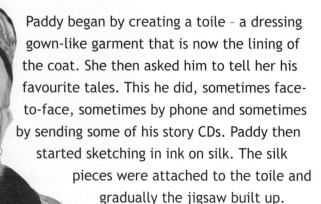

Paddy began by creating a toile – a dressing gown-like garment that is now the lining of the coat. She then asked him to tell her his favourite tales. This he did, sometimes face-to-face, sometimes by phone and sometimes by sending some of his story CDs. Paddy then started sketching in ink on silk. The silk pieces were attached to the toile and gradually the jigsaw built up. Finally, the whole quilted coat was machine-embroidered.

A WORKING PIECE OF FINE ART

Taffy donned the coat for two launch events in 1999, at The Laing Gallery in Tyneside, and the Armitt Collection museum, gallery and library in Ambleside. Since the launch events, he has performed with the Tale Coat in hundreds of schools, hospitals and hospices ... indeed wherever anyone has wanted a story. In October 2001, he even wore it to Buckingham Palace to collect an MBE for services to storytelling and charity.

For the first year after taking possession of the coat, Taffy felt the responsibility of wearing a £4000 piece of textile art, and the coat wore him! He had to remind himself of the original concept of the coat: one of passing control to the audience – a fairly unusual position for most performing artists. The Tale Coat was not a costume, purely an aid to involving audience members in choosing a story. But the more he wore it – whether in schools, at festivals, or even on the street – the more comfortable he felt, and he noted that people's respect for this beautiful work of art grew.

Although now almost twenty years old, the coat remains as exquisite as ever and a continual source of inspiration to Taffy and his audiences.

AUTHOR'S NOTE

The Tale Coat is a working piece of fine art passing some control of the nature and content of the storytelling performance to audience members. While it is possible for art, particularly performance art, to manipulate and control people, it is also possible for art to help democratise and empower people. If, like me, you prefer the latter stance, then please draw inspiration from my ideas.

Teachers and pupils in schools I visited with the Tale Coat have created storytellers' chairs, gardens and garments for themselves to carry the work forward. So please enjoy and draw inspiration from the 19 Tale Coat stories in this collection and run with them in your own way.

Each story in this collection is preceded by a provenance in the belief that stories have legs. I call this, 'The journey of the story to me'. As the stories have been collected over a period of more than 30 years, my memory for some of these sources may be failing. In apologising for this, I invoke a quote from the great Tom Waits: *'A story doesn't have to be true as long as it's entertaining.'*
Hopefully, these are...

Taffy Thomas, MBE
Laureate for Storytelling 2010-12

'As the story concluded, the boy king was sound asleep.'

THE KING'S OWN STORYTELLER

This tale was first told to me by Scots traveller, the late
Duncan Williamson, at his hearthside just north of Edinburgh.

The king and the queen had a son, the prince. Sad it is
to say, but the old king died. Every night, when the boy
prince went to bed, his mother, the queen, told him a
story. She could teach him almost anything just through telling
him a story.

So it was that one night the queen decided to tackle the most
difficult subject of all – mortality. She told her son that she
was very old and the time was approaching when she would
rejoin the king. The prince's eyes filled with tears. He knew his
mother was saying she would soon die. "But if you are dead,
who will tell me my bedtime story?" he asked.

Sadly, the queen told her son that she couldn't help with
that problem but that, on the day she died, the boy would be
crowned king. Encouraged, the boy said that if he was the king
he could have anything he chose. The queen agreed but warned
him he would be remembered by his first decision.

The boy said, "In that case, my first decision will be to create
a new job: the post of the king's own storyteller." Whoever got
the job, he said, would have the task of telling him a bedtime

story every night. There wouldn't be much money but it would be a pleasing job to do ... for that is the way with storytelling.

One night, a few months later, when the prince was still a lad, his mother, the queen, peacefully died. The following day, the young prince was crowned king of the land. His courtiers enquired as to his pronouncement or decision. Confidently, the young king ordered the creation of a new job, the post of the king's own storyteller.

The servants headed for the marketplace: "Oh yea, oh yea, oh yea!" they shouted. "Who wants a job as the king's own storyteller? Anyone wishing to audition for this exciting new post must come to the palace gates at 7.30 this evening."

That evening there was a long queue of storytellers at the palace gates. There were men storytellers, women storytellers, fat storytellers and thin storytellers. The boy king greeted them with a cup of tea, for there is no finer way to greet a visiting storyteller. Then he led them into the stateroom and made them stand around the walls. He placed a storyteller's chair in front of his throne and settled down to listen to their tales.

One by one, the visitors sat in the hot seat and told their best story. Sadly, not one of them was good enough. The boy king thanked them and sent them home. He would have to re-advertise the post.

Now the pronouncement went around the world that there was a new job: the post of the king's own storyteller. Anyone wishing to audition should queue up at the palace gates in one month's time ... for it would take them that long to come from the farthest parts of the world.

A month later, there was an even longer queue at the palace gates. This time there were storytellers with black skins, storytellers with red skins and feathers on their heads, storytellers with yellow skins and pigtails, even storytellers in sealskin anoraks who had made the journey in kayaks. The boy king greeted them all with a meal, for there is no finer way to greet storytellers who have travelled a long way than with a meal. The king led them into the stateroom and made them stand around the walls. He placed a storyteller's chair in front of his throne and settled down to listen to their tales.

One by one, the visitors sat in the hot seat and told their best story. But sadly, not one of them was good enough! The king thanked them and sent them homeward.

The boy king was depressed; he hadn't had a bedtime story since the day his mother died. He decided to do the thing that many people resort to when stressed or depressed – he went for some quiet time in the garden.

As he strolled into the garden with his head down and his eyes filled with tears, he came across the old gardener. Now, the gardener knew the boy king as a master and as a friend, for it was in that very garden that, as a toddler and a young prince, he had taken his first steps and said his first word, "Grass". The gardener gently enquired, "Why are you so sad?" The boy king told his old friend that he hadn't had a bedtime story since his mother died, and couldn't find a replacement storyteller who was good enough.

The old gardener thought that he had some good stories and was probably a little too old for the physical work of gardening. Nothing ventured, nothing gained, so he offered the young king his services as his storyteller. Wisely, the king gratefully said that he would love the gardener to have the job but knew he had to be seen to be fair, for he would be remembered by his first decision. Accordingly, he told the gardener that if he wanted the job, he too must come to the palace gates at 7.30 and audition along with everyone else.

Feeling a little better, the boy king returned to the palace, knowing he would again have the company of his old friend later that day. The gardener went back to work, all the time considering which would be his best story. He decided on 'Jack and the Moneylender', a moral tale some 45 minutes long. Even while working, he was honing the tale.

He finished work early, returned to his cottage to wash and change, for you always have to look your best when telling a story. He arrived at the palace gates in good time to be greeted by the boy king, who excitedly led him through to the stateroom. The king settled on the throne and the gardener sat on the storyteller's chair, facing the king. The old man drew breath and launched into all 45 minutes of 'Jack and the

Moneylender'. At the end of the story, the boy king commended the gardener on his telling, but told him he hadn't got the story quite right. However, as the royal motto was 'If at first you don't succeed, try again', the young king advised the gardener to return the following day, and do just that.

The gardener went back to his cottage, lit the fire and settled in his armchair to practise the story a couple more times before bed. He needed the story to be as tight as a drum skin.

The following day, he continued to practise while trimming the lawn. He again finished work early and washed and changed so that he could arrive at the palace in good time. As before, the boy king relaxed on the throne and the gardener relaxed in the storyteller's chair, ready to do his best. After three-quarters of an hour, the king told the old man that his performance was much improved but that he *still* hadn't got the story quite right. But, believing in the saying 'Third time lucky', he advised the gardener to return the following day and try once more.

The gardener went back to the cottage and set a mirror in front of his armchair. He practised telling the tale using the reflection to devise extravagant facial expressions to enrich his performance.

The following day the gardener worked in the greenhouse pricking out seedlings. From time to time, he practised his telling again, using his reflection in the greenhouse glass. With fingers crossed and quiet confidence, he again washed and changed and made his way to the palace. The boy king wished him luck and again settled on the throne. With some trepidation, the gardener embarked on his story. Fifteen minutes in, the boy king's head was nodding. After 30 minutes, the boy king's eyes were closed. As the story concluded, the boy king was sound asleep. The gardener tiptoed out of the room and home to his cottage. As he walked through the garden he feared the worst. He thought that he had lost the job and, even worse, perhaps his life, for the punishment in those days for upsetting the king was to have your head chopped off.

In the middle of the night, there was a thumping on the cottage door. Fearing the worst the gardener leapt out of bed, put on his boots and clattered down the stairs. Opening the door he found two soldiers and a courtier, who announced that he should go to see the king immediately. The gardener rubbed his neck sadly, dreading the executioner's blade.

He was marched to the palace and straight to the stateroom. The boy king was still asleep on the throne in exactly the same position. As the gardener grew closer, the king opened his eyes and greeted his old friend. "Gardener, I have some great news for you; you will be the king's own storyteller. The job is yours!"

Surprised, the gardener commented that when he had told his best story the king had gone to sleep. He was even more surprised when the king agreed. "You told the story exactly as my mother used to tell it," he said. "That is why I fell so deeply asleep ... and that is why the job is yours."

A WOMAN'S BURDEN

Just before a series of performances for some all-female audiences (the Women's Institute, to be precise), I was lamenting to a Carlisle audience my need for more stories with female protagonists. Over a cup of tea, a random member of the audience gave me this wonderful tale. It's always better to go home with one more story than I arrived with - and it made a nice present for my wife, Chrissy, who truly understood it.

Many years ago, a husband and wife lived on the edge of a forest and they kept goats. However, there were wolves in the forest so they built a tower for safety. Every night, they had to carry the goats up the tower and every morning they had to carry them down.

The drums were beating on the border and the husband had to go away to war as men have had to do since time immemorial, leaving his wife to manage as best as she could. At this time, they had only one goat. Every night the wife had to carry the goat up the tower and every morning carry it down to graze – every night and every morning for seven years, and a goat can grow a lot in seven years.

After seven years, the husband returned from the war. He was one of the lucky ones. The wife was pleased to see him back but said, "Tonight you can carry the goat up the tower."

The husband, pleased to be home, was delighted to do this job. However, when he tried to pick up the goat, it had grown so much he couldn't lift it. Watching him struggle, the wife laughed and pushed him out of the way. She scooped the goat into her arms and set off up the tower.

Amazed, the husband asked, "Why can you do that, if I can't?"

The wife simply replied, "That's the way it is with a women's burden, it gets a little bit bigger each day, and we don't notice the change!"

'Every night the wife had to carry the goat up the tower...'

THE TIGER AND THE FOUR ANTELOPE

Surprisingly, although this is an African story, it came to me from the mouth of Scots traveller, the late Duncan Williamson.

One morning, a tiger woke hungry and fancied a nice juicy meal of antelope meat. Off he travelled and found a small herd of four antelope. One of those would be his meal for the day. He then realised that the antelope had sharp teeth, pointy horns and heavy hooves. In short, they could bite him, prong him and kick him to death.

The tiger decided that discretion was the best option. He lay and waited until one antelope moved a hundred metres from the herd. This would be his victim. However, with only a hundred metres between the lone antelope and his herd, the other three could still race over to kick, bite and prong. The tiger had to come up with a plan to further separate his victim.

He crept up to the one on his own, but passing close enough to the other three to pretend to listen to them as he went by.

He asked the lone antelope whether the other three were its friends. The lone antelope said they were very good friends. The tiger stated that this was not so, as when he passed the group of three, they had been talking about the other one, saying it was fat and ugly. The lone antelope said, in that case, it would have nothing to do with the others ever again, and moved a further hundred metres away from the herd.

The lone antelope was now fair game. The tiger sprinted up, pounced, killed and pulled the antelope limb from limb, gorging on the flesh.

Having eaten so much meat, the tiger felt sleepy. He nodded off to sleep, happily thinking that, if he woke up hungry again, there were still three antelope remaining.

Sometime later, the tiger woke up hungry. He went and found the 'gang of three', but remembered that they, too, had sharp teeth, sharp pointy horns and heavy hooves. He lay and waited

'Becoming even more devious, the tiger crept around behind one of the antelope and nipped his backside.'

until one moved just a hundred metres from the herd. For his own safety, the tiger decided to use the same tactic: he approached the lone antelope while passing very close to the other two, so as to appear to be listening to them. He asked the solitary antelope if the three were friends. The antelope replied that they were, and that there used to be four but one hadn't come home the previous night.

The tiger licked the dried blood from his whiskers and said, innocently, that he wondered what had happened to that one. Then, the tiger surprised the antelope by saying that the three of them couldn't really be friends, as he had just heard the other two saying that the lone antelope was too old to keep up with the herd. They were thinking of finding a new antelope – younger and trendier – to be in their herd.

The antelope said, if that were the case, he would have nothing to do with them ever again, and he moved another hundred metres from the herd. Now he was fair game.

The tiger sprinted over, pounced, killed and gorged itself on the flesh of the antelope. Having eaten all this meat, the tiger felt sleepy, so once again he went to rest, happy in the knowledge that, if he woke up hungry again, he could still find the remaining two antelope.

So it was that, later, the tiger woke up hungry and located the two surviving antelope. But he was faced with a problem: they, too, had sharp teeth, pointy horns and heavy hooves and, if he was caught between them, they could bite, prong and kick him to death. He needed to come up with a cunning plan to separate them, but he couldn't say that one was talking about the other because they were only the two of them left.

Becoming even more devious, the tiger crept around behind one of the antelope and nipped his backside.

The antelope jumped, "Who did that?"

By then the tiger had crept around behind the other antelope and nipped at that one's bottom.

This one also jumped, "Who did that?"

The tiger had slid away to a safe distance, so the antelope blamed each other, locked horns and started to battle. As they tired of this, they separated, one walking off a hundred metres in one direction and one a hundred metres in the other. They were now both fair game. The tiger picked the weakest, pounced, killed and gorged himself on the flesh and blood. Feeling, sleepy, he nodded off, knowing that when he woke up hungry, there was still one antelope, on his own, that he could eat whenever he wanted, and that is exactly what the tiger did.

POSTSCRIPT

If you have a good friend, there will always be someone who will be jealous and who will gossip and try to separate you. So don't necessarily believe gossip: try to stick with your friends and trust them, for unity is strength.

DAVY AND THE FISH

Twenty years ago, a teenage Shropshire storyteller called Amy Douglas trailed me, hoping to learn some storytelling skills and to find some new stories. Eventually, I set her a challenge: I refused to give her another story unless she gave me a new tale. This is the gem that challenge produced. My version is much informed by two years' work as an inshore fisherman: one year in East Suffolk and, more importantly, one year as crew for old salt Tommy Morrissey in Padstow, Cornwall.

D avy hated fish. He didn't like the taste of it, he didn't like the smell of it and he didn't like the slimy way it felt. Which was unfortunate, because the only job that Davy could find, at 18 years of age, was working for an old fisherman.

Every day, when they went to sea and the skipper dumped the catch on the deck, Davy's job was cutting off fish heads and taking out their guts – the squidgy bits in the middle. Davy hated that part of the work.

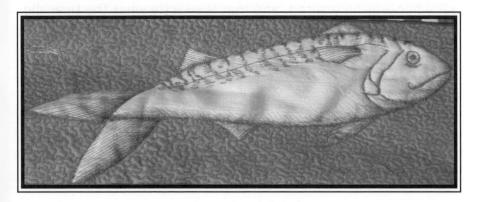

One fine day at sea, the skipper dumped a mackerel on the deck for gutting. Davy admired its beautiful stripes and bright eye. When he felt the fish wriggling in his hands he couldn't bring himself to kill it. So he hid it behind his back and, when he thought the skipper wasn't looking, he slipped it back over the side of the boat into the sea. He gave it its life.

But the skipper had seen and there was a terrible row. The old man pointed out that he didn't go to sea every day, getting soaked to the skin catching fish to scrape a living, only for the boy to throw them back.

Davy stood before the mast whistling. Now you never whistle on a fishing boat, for if you do, you're either whistling up the wind or you're whistling up the devil. This made the skipper even more furious. In fact, he sacked Davy on the spot, telling him that when they returned to the port, he must leave the boat and never set foot on it again.

Davy was half-glad and he was half-sad. He was half-glad because he hated the job anyway, and he was half-sad because he knew he was going to have to go home and tell his wife he was out of work again.

He left the boat, climbing the ladder to the quayside, his eyes filled with tears and the corners of his mouth turned down. On the walk home, Davy realised he'd got company: there was a strange man walking beside him, leading a black and white Friesian cow. If Davy had looked carefully he would have noticed two little horns on the top of the stranger's head and a red tail sticking out of the back of his trousers. Of course, it was Old Nick, Old Scratch … the devil himself!

The devil asked why Davy looked so sad. Davy told the stranger that he had lost his job and that he was going to have to go home and tell his wife … he was in big trouble.

The devil told Davy that if he owned the black and white cow he wouldn't be out of work because the cow gave the richest and creamiest milk there has ever been: Davy and his wife could make butter, cheese and ice-cream and open a teashop – something they'd always fancied doing.

The devil made a bargain with Davy, telling him that he could borrow the cow for three years. However, when he returned to collect it he would ask Davy three questions. If Davy couldn't answer them, he would be thrown over the devil's shoulder and carried away to burn in the fires of hell.

To Davy, three years seemed a long way off. Besides, at the age of 18, he thought himself invincible. He shook hands with the devil and the bargain was struck. The devil handed Davy the rope, which was tied around the cow's neck, and headed for home. As the devil did a double somersault and disappeared through a crack in the earth, Davy thought he would never set eyes on him again.

Davy's wife was looking out through the kitchen window. When she saw her husband walking up the lane, leading a black and white cow, she was amazed. Davy had brought home friends

'If Davy had looked carefully he would have noticed two little horns on the top of the stranger's head, and a red tail sticking out of the back of his trousers.'

before, he'd brought home fish before, but he'd never before brought home a cow.

She rushed out to meet him and asked what was going on. Proudly, Davy told her that the cow gave the richest and creamiest milk there's ever been, and they were going to open a teashop, for he had packed in the fishing.

The news of Davy and his wife's teashop soon spread – like the butter itself – and they did very well.

But three years to the day after the bargain was struck with the devil, Davy was in the teashop mopping the floor, with just one customer – a stranger – sitting in the corner.

Suddenly, there was a flash of blue light and there appeared Old Nick, Old Scratch ... the devil himself. He'd polished his skin up bright red and sharpened his hooves and his tail specially.

He looked menacingly at Davy, telling him he had come to collect the cow but, even worse, he had three questions that Davy had to answer. If he couldn't answer them, he would be getting a guided tour of Hades.

He asked if Davy was ready to answer the questions. But, before Davy could utter a word, the stranger in the corner answered that Davy was ready and that the devil had just asked the first question.

Getting slightly niggled, the devil asked if the stranger in the corner would butt out. Quickly, the stranger retorted that he wouldn't, and that the devil had now asked his second question.

Irritably, the devil asked who this interfering stranger was. The stranger replied that he was the King of the Fish. Three years ago Davy had thrown him back over the side of the boat, saving his life, and now he had come to repay Davy for his kindness. Not only this, but the devil had just asked his third and final question.

The devil realised he had been outwitted and, in a tantrum, stamped his hoof on the ground, making a hoof print in the concrete, and stormed out of the teashop. He was in such a sulk that he clean forgot to collect his cow.

As far as I know, Davy and his wife are still there, so if you're ever in a teashop by the seaside, have a glance around the floor and, if you can spot a hoof print in the concrete, you're in the teashop that Davy and his wife are running to this very day.

SINGING TO THE MOON

SINGING TO THE MOON

My friend, East Anglian storyteller Huw Lupton, gave me this tale many years ago. It has proved useful for many school assemblies and festival church services, including sacred stories at Jonesburough, the US national storytelling festival in 2001.

RIDDLE

Q: What has been around for millions of years but is never more than a month old?

A: The moon.

One evening in the rainforest, Bird was singing to Moon. The singing woke Monkey, who was sleeping up a coconut tree. Monkey was furious. He grabbed a coconut and threw it at Bird. Bird ducked and the coconut fell to the ground almost hitting Snake. Snake was scared and slithered into a hole in the ground. Mouse lived in the hole in the ground. Mouse shot out of the hole and ran into the village.

Woman was walking with a bucket to fetch water. Woman was frightened of Mouse. Woman jumped up on to a log and the bucket flew into the air. The king's son was just walking by. The bucket hit him on the head. The king was furious. "Who threw the bucket at my son?" he asked.

The people of the tribe said, "It was Woman."

The king said, "Bring me Woman." He asked Woman, "Why did you throw the bucket at my son?"

Woman said, "I was frightened of Mouse."

The king said, "Bring me Mouse." He asked Mouse, "Why did you frighten Woman so that she threw the bucket at my son?"

Mouse said, "I was frightened of Snake."

The king said, "Bring me Snake." He asked Snake, "Why did you frighten Mouse, who frightened Woman so that she threw the bucket at my son?"

Snake said, "I was scared because Monkey threw a coconut at me."

The king said, "Bring me Monkey." He asked Monkey, "Why did you throw the coconut at Snake so that Snake frightened Mouse who frightened Woman so that she threw the bucket at my son?"

Monkey said, "I threw the coconut at Bird because Bird woke me up."

The king said, "Bring me Bird." He asked Bird, "Why did you wake Monkey so that he threw the coconut at Snake who frightened Mouse who frightened Woman so that she threw the bucket at my son?"

Bird said, "I was so happy, I was singing to Moon."

The king said, "Who put Moon up there?"

The people said, "It was God."

The king said, "Bring me God."

So all the people of the tribe, in fact everyone on earth, set out to find God. And people all over the world have been finding God ever since.

THE STANHOPE FAIRIES

In 1991 I was the North Pennines Storyteller in Residence. While in this role, I met a dear friend in Weardale, a farmer's wife called Maude Coulthard. Maude, who is known for telling jokes at Methodist teas, passed on this jewel of a tale, which was of special interest to me as a collector of riddles.

In Weardale, County Durham, there are several places where there are strange holes in the ground. The Weardale folk never look into these holes for they know they are fairy holes and, if they peer into the holes and the king of the fairies should see them, he will come at midnight and spirit them away.

There was one young girl, about eight years old, from Eastgate, who was a farmer's daughter. She was desperate to see the fairies at the Eastgate fairy holes. So, one day, when her father and mother were busy on the land, she slipped away and ran towards the fairy holes. As she got closer she could hear the jingling of bells and the clip-clopping of hooves. She sat on the edge of a hole, peered in and saw lots of tiny horses with hooves and bells around the saddle. But the king of the fairies looked up and saw her.

The girl jumped up in terror and ran back to the farm to tell her father what she had done. He called her a silly little goose and told her that the king of the fairies would come at midnight and spirit her away unless she went to bed really early and kept completely silent so that the fairies did not find her.

That night, at six o'clock, the father shut all the chickens and ducks in a shed so there was no clucking and quacking. He stopped all the clocks in the house so there was no tick-ticking and the whole family retired to bed early.

At midnight, the farmer heard the jingling of bells and the clip-clopping of hooves. Knowing it would be the approaching fairies he kept completely silent. However, he had forgotten that his daughter had a pet dog that slept beside her bed. The dog pricked up its ears and, hearing the jingling of bells and the clip-clopping of hooves, let out a sharp bark.

Now the fairies knew which room to go to. They bundled the little girl into a blanket and took her away with them back to the fairy holes.

When the farmer awoke in the morning he was distressed to find his daughter gone. What could he do?

He knew that, in Stanhope, there was a gypsy woman who lived in a beautiful painted caravan. Perhaps, if he visited her, she could help.

So, that very morning, he walked from Eastgate to Stanhope, a distance of some three and a half miles. He approached the caravan and knocked on the wooden half door. A thin reedy voice bade him enter. He climbed the three steps into the caravan and found the gypsy woman sitting by the stove making clothes pegs. She asked what he wanted and the farmer explained what had happened to his daughter.

The old woman proffered her right hand and told him that, if he crossed her palm with silver, she could help. The farmer put a hand into his pocket, pulled out a £20 note and pressed it into the gypsy's outstretched hand.

The old woman told him that he must go to the fairy holes himself, wearing a sprig of rowan in his hat for good luck. Furthermore, he would have to take with him three presents – but he would have to answer three riddles to find out the nature of these presents. He had to take: a chicken without a bone; a light that couldn't be lit; and a part of an animal's flesh that could be taken without a drop of blood being drawn.

The farmer couldn't immediately answer any of these riddles, but did know where to find a rowan tree on the fellside. He thanked the old lady and set out to collect his sprig of rowan, for he needed all the luck he could find.

Halfway up the hill he met a tramp who was starving. The tramp begged an apple, a lump of cheese and half a stottie cake from the farmer. Thanking the farmer, he offered his help.

The farmer told him that he needed a chicken without a bone. The tramp explained that this was, of course, an egg.

Delighted, the farmer headed towards the chicken shed to collect his egg.

By the chicken house, a kestrel was diving on a blackbird. The farmer shooed the kestrel away, saving the blackbird's life. Gratefully, the blackbird offered his help. So the farmer told the bird that he needed to find a light that didn't have to be lit.

'Halfway up the hill he met a tramp who was starving.'

The blackbird informed him that this was, of course, a glow-worm.

So off the farmer headed, towards the wood, to trap this insect.

On the edge of the wood, a naughty boy was throwing stones at a rabbit. The farmer sent the boy home to his mother, so saving the rabbit's life. In return for his kind deed, the rabbit offered the farmer help.

The farmer told him that he needed a part of an animal's flesh without a drop of blood being drawn. Immediately, the rabbit explained that, if he climbed Softly Bank, which is the hill from Weardale into Teesdale, the farmer might find a lizard on the rocks. If he pulled the lizard's tail it would come off without a drop of blood being drawn and the lizard would grow a new one.

So the farmer climbed Softly Bank and, indeed, discovered a lizard scampering on the rocks. He tweaked the lizard's tail and it came off in his hand.

Armed with the tail, the insect and the egg, and wearing the sprig of rowan, the farmer set off back to Eastgate to the fairy holes. He presented these gifts to the king of the fairies who was so delighted that he told the farmer his daughter could return safely with him to the farm.

And the daughter was so pleased to be going home that she promised her parents that she would never slip off again without them knowing her whereabouts.

THE CLEVER WISH

Irish-American storyteller, Patrick Ryan, used to use my Grasmere home as a breakfast stop when returning from Ireland via the Stranraer ferry to his home in London. He ate my fridge empty but left this tale as fine payment.

There was once a man, and he was desperately unlucky. He had no food and no money. He and his wife also longed for a child of their own. But however hard they tried, no baby was born to them. And if this wasn't bad enough, he had a mother who was completely blind. No food, no money, no baby and a blind mother. What could he do?

The man thought long and hard. He had to find a way to feed his wife, his mother and himself. So he borrowed a gun and went out to the woods to shoot a rabbit, for he thought he could make rabbit stew. Although rabbit stew is not a great dinner, it's better than no dinner at all.

He was just looking for a rabbit to shoot when there was a flash of white. He parted the bushes and there in the bush, with its hoof stuck in a trap, was a unicorn: a snow-white horse with one long golden spiral horn. The man was considering the possibility of unicorn stew when the unicorn turned and spoke to him. "If you spare my life and set me free, I can give you one wish." Instantly, our hero thought of money. The unicorn sadly shook its head and said that money wasn't the answer to everything, and didn't necessarily bring happiness.

If his first thought was money, his second thought was for food, his third thought was for a baby and his fourth thought was for his mother's eyesight to be restored.

So, you see, this story presents a dilemma: what should he wish for: Money? Food? A baby? Or his mother's sight?

Well, the story is called 'The clever wish'. So, the man freed the magical beast, then wished that his mother could see him and his wife rocking their baby in a golden cradle.

SUDDENLY there was a flash of blue light and the man found himself next to his wife, rocking a baby in a golden cradle. His mother was standing by the cradle smiling, for she could now see. But a baby doesn't need a golden cradle, so that very afternoon the man sold it and, with the money, bought enough food to feed his family for the rest of their days.

'He parted the bushes and there in the bush, with its hoof stuck in a trap, was a unicorn.'

THE LEGEND OF THE DEVIL'S BRIDGE

In 1995, when undertaking a year as South Lakeland's Storyteller in Residence, I met George Harrison of Kirkby Lonsdale, who includes this story in his historical town walk. He told it to me on the very bridge featured in the story and showed me the devil's handprint in one of the slabs. Strangely the same legend exists for similarly named bridges in Wales and Italy. How can that be?

If you visit the fair town of Kirkby Lonsdale, you can see evidence of the many markets that used to be held in the town. The evidence is in the street names. There's Horsemarket, where they used to sell horses, of course, and Swinemarket where they used to sell ... yes, you've guessed it ... pigs. (Although once, when relating this tale, I enquired of the audience as to what might have been sold in Swinemarket. A toddler, sitting on his mother's knee at the back, retorted that they might have sold children! His mother went bright red: now we all knew what she called the small lad!) There is also the market square in Kirkby Lonsdale where they still hold a market every week.

Every Thursday, a farmer's wife travelled from Cowan Bridge, on the Yorkshire border, to Kirkby Lonsdale market to sell bread. She came with her dog, a little fat Yorkshire terrier called Charlie. Now, Charlie the dog's legs were so short, they only just reached the ground.

On the way, they crossed the small wooden footbridge over the river Lune. Well-travelled readers might, at this point, be thinking that there isn't a small wooden footbridge over the Lune ... and they'd be right. However, this story explains why this is the case.

The farmer's wife set up the stall in the market square. As she started trading, it started to rain. (It does a bit of that on market day in Kirkby Lonsdale.) It rained all day but she still sold all of her bread buns except one. She popped this bun in her bag, shut up shop and, with her dog, started the homeward journey, for she had her husband and the beasts on the farm to feed on her return.

When they had reached the banks of the river Lune, she discovered there had been a flash flood and the small wooden footbridge had been washed away.

Disconsolately, she gazed into the grey swirling water, wondering how she could cross the river. She knew that if she attempted to swim or wade through the angry stream, she would drown and her body swept down through Lancaster.

She could sense something on her right-hand side. She glanced around, there was a crack and a flash of light and there stood a small red man with horns, hooves and a pointed tail.

"Well," she thought, "He's not a local!"

'Old Nick offered to build her a bridge right there and then.'

Old Nick, Old Scratch, the devil himself, for that's who it was, asked the farmer's wife why she was in such distress. She retorted that she needed a bridge building across the river to enable her return home.

Old Nick offered to build her a bridge right there and then, in just one night, but only if the farmer's wife made a bargain with him, because that's the way it is with the devil.

The bargain was that if he built the bridge, the soul of the first living creature to cross the bridge must accompany him back to hell.

The farmer's wife glanced down at Charlie the dog and had an idea. She shook hands with the devil and the bargain was struck.

The farmer's wife and the dog then curled up under a tree to catch some sleep while Old Nick donned his apron and went up on to the fellside collecting rocks. In fact, he collected so many rocks that his apron strings broke.

If you doubt my tale, then remember, you don't have to travel too far east from Lunesdale before you enter Kingsdale, and in Kingsdale, to this day, there's a semi circle of rocks on the fellside called the Devil's Apron. Even the Yorkshire folk who live nearby don't know why these rocks are called the Devil's Apron, but the storytellers know ... and now so do you.

The devil repaired his apron and eventually collected enough rock and stone to build a fine bridge, which still known throughout the North of England as the Devil's Bridge. His work completed, he woke the farmer's wife and reminded her of the bargain.

She put her hands in a bag, removed the sole remaining bread roll and waved it under the nose of Charlie the dog. Charlie sniffed and got a scent of a breakfast. The farmer's wife then rolled the bun across the bridge and Charlie, who in his mind's eye became a greyhound, shot after it.

Triumphantly, the farmer's wife indicated to Old Nick that the dog was the first living creature to cross the bridge.

Old Nick, realising he had been outwitted, flew into a tantrum and ran to the middle of the bridge, shaking his fist and screaming abuse. In his temper, he slammed his right claw on the right-hand parapet of the bridge.

So, if you visit the Devil's Bridge in Kirkby Lonsdale and walk across it towards the town, pause in the middle and look to your right: you will clearly see a handprint, claw marks and all. I know this to be true because the last time I visited the bridge, I found the handprint and put my hand in it. Remarkably, it fitted exactly. However, I'm assured that neither the devil nor Charlie the dog have been seen in Kirkby Lonsdale from that day to this.

THE CAT FISHERS

Here is another delight, brought to the Lake District by Scottish traveller, the late Duncan Williamson, on one of his many visits.

I f you look over the bridge into the River Rothay at Grasmere, you might spot brown trout or sea trout. If you walk along the riverbank, you may well come to an old barn. Now, that barn is the home of two pussycats. One of these cats is an old black cat, and he's a bit like me, because he's a storyteller. The other cat is a little white kitten – she's young and she's fast.

Every night, the old black cat and the little white kitten curl up in the hay in the barn, and the old black cat tells the little white kitten stories. Those stories are usually about how good the old black cat was when he was her age, because those are the kind of stories that parents and teachers tell you. (In truth, they probably used to be naughtier than you, but if you want those stories you have to go and ask your grandparents!)

The little white kitten got fed up with the old black cat boasting about how good he used to be. So one night the kitten said, "I don't want a story tonight. We'll go straight to sleep."

The old black cat said that this was a pity, as tonight he was going to tell her how good he used to be at fishing. Then, in the morning, he was planning to take her down to the riverbank and teach her how to fish.

The kitten said he should skip the story but still give her the fishing lesson on the morrow.

The following morning, the two cats yawned, stretched and padded out of the barn and down to the riverbank. The black cat demonstrated that, to tickle a trout, she should put her paw in the water with her claws out, and when the fish swam over her paw she should flick it out on to the bank.

He demonstrated this several times and then announced that she could fish in that spot. He, however, was going a bit farther downstream. He knew somewhere better to fish, but wasn't prepared to give away all his secrets at once.

Excited, the little white kitten approached the water's edge: she put her paw in the water with her claws out, and as soon as a fish swam over them, she triumphantly flicked it out on to the bank next to her. She was proud she had caught her first fish, because she was young and fast.

Downstream, the old black cat wasn't doing quite so well. He was older and slower. He put his paw in the water with his claws out, but when a fish swam over his paw, he was too slow and, by the time he tried to flick it out on to the bank, the fish was away and safe under a stone. Although he fished the whole of the morning and the afternoon, he couldn't catch anything; he was just too slow.

As the sun started to dip behind the fell, he gave up and went back to see how the little white kitten had fared. Seeing him coming up the bank, the kitten stood proudly over her catch and arched her back in a threatening manner. This was her first fish and she was proud, and planned to savour it for supper.

She called to the old black cat, asking him how he had done. On hearing he had been unsuccessful, because he was too old and slow, the kitten started to laugh. The old cat pointed out that, one day, she too would grow old, and anyway his lack of success didn't matter because she had caught a fish and they could share it.

The kitten pointed out that it was her first fish and she had no plans to share it. So the old black cat reminded her that he had taught her how to catch it, and that every night he told her stories, so perhaps now she should share something. The kitten again stated she had no plans to share.

And so the argument began. The two cats howled, yowled and hissed at each other. They made such a row, they awoke old Daddy Fox in his den on the fellside, for the fox hunts at night and sleeps during the day. He came down the fellside to investigate.

As soon as he spotted the fish by the kitten, he licked his chops, for Daddy Fox liked to eat fish, too. He complained that the cats had woken him up and asked what their problem was.

The old black cat explained that they were arguing about which cat should eat the fish for supper.

Daddy Fox offered to be the decider. First he asked who had caught the fish.

'While they were concentrating on their musical skills, they failed to notice as Daddy Fox stuck out his paw, flicking the fish towards himself.'

The kitten proudly stated that she had caught it and so it was hers. The black cat said that he had been her teacher and so deserved his share.

Daddy Fox realised the situation was more complex than it had first seemed, but he had a cunning plan to resolve the dispute. He pointed out that they had quarrelled for so long, the moon was out in the sky. Now, we all know that cats sing to the moon. Daddy Fox's idea was a singing competition: the two cats should sing to the moon, and whichever sang the best would be rewarded with the fish supper.

The old black cat boasted that this would be him, as he knew all the old arias and folksongs, and what the young kitten called music – pop and rock – was just a noise.

The two cats put their heads back, drew breath, and started to sing: "MEEEEEOW, MEEEEEOW, MEEEEEEEEEEEEOW."

While they were concentrating on their musical skills, they failed to notice as Daddy Fox stuck out his paw, flicking the fish towards himself. He seized the fish and took it back to his den to feed his vixen and his cubs.

The two cats sang on for another half an hour: "MEEEEEOW, MEEEEEOW, MEEEEEEEEEEEEOW".

When they stopped singing, they looked down but there was no sign of a fish ... and no sign of the fox. All they could do was return to the barn and go to bed hungry.

That was one night when the old black cat didn't tell any stories at all.

THE SEA MORGAN

The shores of these islands are abound with stories of mermaids and mermen, and this strange one comes from my native Somerset. It is special to me as my great grandfather, who I never met, was a seaman sailing out of the North Somerset port of Watchet. The story was told to me by octogenarian West Country storyteller, Ruth Tongue.

One day, a fisherman came from Watchet to see St Audries Bay. As he walked along the shore, he heard singing coming from the sea. It was the sea morgan, playing in the shallows with their children.

Hearing the sound of the fisherman's boots approaching, the sea morgan swam for deep water. However, they accidentally left a baby morgan splashing around in a rock pool, where the fisherman discovered her.

The fisherman and his wife were still grieving, for they had not long since laid a baby daughter to rest in Watchet Churchyard. On finding the baby morgan, the fisherman thought that if he carried her home, his wife might take to it and they could bring the little one up as their own. Gently, he lifted the baby from the pool, cradled her in his arms and bore her home.

His wife took to the little one straight away and, as the fisherman had hoped, they brought her up as their own. But when the baby became a toddler, she was always looking for puddles to splash in and she could never get her hair dry, for that is the way with sea morgan.

'As he walked along the shore, he heard singing coming from the sea.'

Unfortunately, they had a nosy neighbour, a very strict, puritanical sort of woman. One day the mean-spirited neighbour turned on the toddler. "You can never get your hair dry, and you're always looking for water, and that ain't Christian!"

She told all the men in nearby Staple and Doniford that she had a witch child living next door, and these men, being equally puritanical, believed their duty was to destroy the witch child.

They sharpened their blades, put on their boots and marched down the road, filled with righteous malice.

At the tiny fisherman's cottage, the kitchen door was open. The toddler heard the sound of the marching men and cluttering blades, but she also heard the sound of singing coming from the sea – the sea morgan were returning to rescue their own. The toddler ran a big loop around the advancing men, down to the beach and dived into the ocean.

When the fisherman returned home from sea that night, he couldn't find the child anywhere. He and his wife walked the length of the beach, but the toddler was gone.

Every day, for the rest of their lives, they walked up and down the beach, hoping to find the child. And, though sometimes they heard the sound of singing coming from the waves, they never set eyes on the little one again nor held her in their arms. For she was safe with her own.

So the next time you see a child splashing in a puddle, or a young girl who can't get her hair dry, beware ... she may be a sea morgan!

INNA AND THE EEL

During the 1980s, a surprise knock on my cottage door heralded the arrival of Illinois storyteller, Jim May, holding a coconut. He had come to see me direct from his appearance at the Hawaiian Storytelling Festival, bringing me a coconut and this story. Thanks, Jim!

O n the island of Maui lived a young girl called Inna. Men were few in her tiny village and visitors rare. Living with her family, Inna had chores and her daily duty was to take a leather bucket up to the river and collect water – water to drink, water for washing and water for cooking.

One day, Inna stood in the river scooping water into the leather bucket, when she spotted a long, dark shape slithering upstream. Inna shivered. She knew it was an eel, and she didn't like eels! The eel slithered against Inna's leg and she shivered

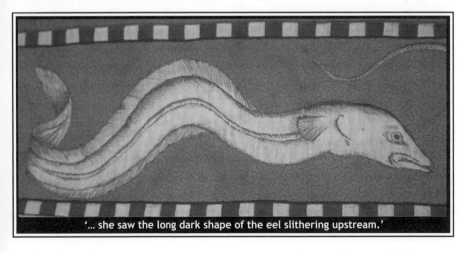

'... she saw the long dark shape of the eel slithering upstream.'

even harder. Just then, the eel popped his head out of the water and smiled. Inna realised the eel wanted to play. He wanted to play tig.

Inna ran upstream and tigged the eel. The eel slithered between her legs and swam downstream. Inna ran downstream and tigged the eel. Again the eel slithered between her legs and turned upstream.

Just then, a parrot cried out from a tree on the riverbank. While Inna was looking at the beautiful bird, the eel slithered out onto a mud bank and magically transformed into a handsome young man. When Inna saw the young man lying there on the bank, he beckoned her towards him.

Excitedly, Inna crossed the river and spent the rest of the afternoon with this handsome stranger. When Inna returned

'Just then, a parrot cried out from a tree on the riverbank.'

home late with the water, her mother wondered why she was a little different.

Somehow the chore of fetching the water wasn't quite so punishing now. Every day, Inna would run to the river; every day she would play with the eel. And on the good days, the eel changed into the handsome young man, and it was the happiest summer of Inna's life.

Towards the end of the summer, Inna was lying on the beach in the sunshine with the young man when he shocked her by telling her: "The rainy season will soon be here. This year it will be so bad that most of your people will die, but you can save them."

Inna pointed out that she was just a young girl. So what could she do? The young man told her that, before long, she would be going about her business collecting water when she would suddenly hear the rustle of the wind through the trees. This would soon be followed by the patter of raindrops on the river. If she looked downstream she would spot the long dark shape of the eel, slithering upstream for the last time. To save her people she must kill it.

The young man told her exactly what she should do.

As soon as the flooding river covered the beach, she must pick up a conch shell, knock the end off on a rock and, using the shell as a trumpet, blow a warning to her village that the floods were imminent.

She must then pick up a piece of flint and hone the edge of the shell until it is razor sharp. By now, the eel would be just under the surface, midstream. Inna was told she must wade out into the river with the shell and with it she must cut off the eel's head. She must then carry the severed head back to the river bank and bury it in the mud of the beach.

Although Inna was horrified with this responsibility, the young man reassured her that, if she revisited the spot where she'd buried the eel's head, something would happen that would save her people. Inna hoped the day would never come when she would have to kill her love.

A few weeks later, Inna was collecting the water in the river when she felt a whisper of the southern wind followed by the patter of raindrops. The shower became a torrent and the river started to flood. Inna hoped the eel would not show up, but dutifully she grabbed a conch shell, knocked off the end and blew a warning of the flood to her village. Shaking, she saw the long dark shape of the eel slithering upstream. Remembering her instructions, Inna picked up a piece of flint and started to hone the edge of the shell until it was razor sharp.

The eel lurked just under the surface, midstream, and bravely Inna waded over, clutching the shell above her head and swept the shell down. The flood turned blood red as Inna cut the head from the eel. Tenderly, she carried the severed head back to the mud of the beach. Then she scooped a hole and buried it.

She returned home with her bucket of water and her eyes filled with tears. In the village, many people were also in tears as, on the first day of the flood, most of their crops had been destroyed and they feared starvation.

A few days later, Inna returned to the muddy beach. Where she had buried the eel's head, a tiny green shoot had appeared. Inna tended this shoot daily and it grew into a tall, straight tree, bearing three or four large brown hairy nuts. They were coconuts – the first coconuts that had ever grown on this planet.

When Inna climbed the tree and picked one of the nuts, she bore it safely to earth and opened it. She discovered that it contained milk to drink and food to eat – a complete natural packed lunch in a hard shell.

Thanks to these nuts, Inna's family were the only survivors in that tiny village.

To this day, the people of the South Sea Islands never go fishing in their canoes unless they take with them a couple of coconuts in case they are swept out of their vessel onto a distant shore.

POSTSCRIPT

In case you doubt this tale, the next time you take the hairy tuft off a coconut, look carefully and you can see three black dots: two eyes and mouth – the face of the eel.

KING OF THE BIRDS

*I learned this story by osmosis somewhere in my 60-year journey - probably
even before I was a storyteller. When told in a school classroom, it is
guaranteed to cheer and can help raise the self-esteem of even the
smallest, quietest child. I added the traditional rhyme conclusion, basing it
on the final verse in a Steeleye Span song called 'Hunting the Wren'.*

The birds of the air were discussing which of them
should be king. In this situation, it is quite usual that
one steps forward as self-appointed leader.

So it was that the golden eagle decided he was the biggest
and best and strutted around boasting and bragging: "Me, I'm
the biggest, I'm the best." The trouble was he became too big
for his beak and the other birds tired of his boasting and posing.

The chattering magpies sought the assistance of the wise
old owl. They asked if the owl could devise a plan to bring the
eagle down a perch or two.

The owl decided that the following day there should be a
competition to see which bird could fly the highest. Hearing of
this, the eagle bragged even more. He mocked the competition
as a waste of time, for he was biggest and best and could fly
the highest.

The following day, all the birds lined up on a nearby ridge.
At one end of the line was the hawk posse - the kestrel, the
sparrowhawk, the osprey and, of course, the golden eagle.

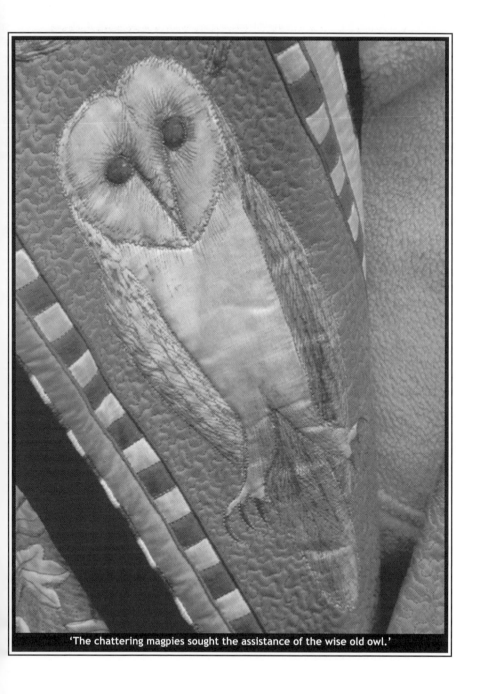

'The chattering magpies sought the assistance of the wise old owl.'

Next to the hawks, the big black birds fell into line – the rook, the raven, the jackdaw and the crow.

Next to them, the blackbird and thrush and, of course, the chattering magpies.

A colourful line of robins, blue tits and finches placed themselves between the blackbirds and an enormous line of sparrows. At the far end of the line was the smallest of all – little Jenny Wren.

No sooner had they formed up in line than the eagle started strutting around and boasting, deriding the competition as a waste of time.

The owl decided to step in. Moving along the line, he whispered something in the ear of little Jenny Wren – a cunning plan. Nodding, she tiptoed around the back of the line. The eagle was so busy boasting and posing, he didn't notice as the wren climbed on to his back and nuzzled down in the feathers.

The owl took three steps backwards and pronounced, "On your marks ... get set ... GO!"

The sky was black with birds. The sparrows were the first to tire and drifted down to land.

Soon after, the coloured birds – the robins, blue tits and finches – became weary and landed.

Even the magpies, the thrush, the blackbird and the big black birds – the rook, the raven, the jackdaw and the crow – wearied and glided back to earth.

Yet high in the sky, the hawks had found a thermal and continued to soar.

Eventually, even they tired and the kestrel, sparrowhawk and osprey gracefully glided down, leaving one speck high in the sky ... the speck that was the golden eagle.

The hawks commented that although the eagle had been boastful, he had merely told the truth, as he was the strongest and had flown the highest.

No sooner had the hawks decided this, than the eagle began to tire and commenced his descent. On his back, little Jenny Wren felt the change in altitude and launched herself upwards. Just for a moment, the eagle was coming down while the wren still climbed upwards.

On landing, the eagle of course continued to boast that the competition had been a waste of time as he had proved himself the biggest and best. But the other birds pointed to the tiniest speck still high in the sky – the speck that was little Jenny Wren.

Drifting down, she was encircled by the rest of the birds, who pointed out that she was the king of the birds – for although she was the smallest in size, she was the biggest in wit.

The wren, the wren, is king of the birds
Saint Stephen's Day she was stuck in the furze
Although she was little, her wit it was great
If you boast like an eagle, you may yet share his fate!

SEDNA, PRINCESS OF THE SEA

I researched this story many years ago, while involved with a youth arts project at the Brewery Arts Centre in Kendal, entitled 'The Whale'. Most British stories I found were about hunting whales and slaughtering them. I had to visit the culture of the Inuit people to find this creation myth. My official right to tell it was gained when, after telling it in a tiny Lake District pub, I observed a member of the audience smiling. He had high cheek bones and slightly olive skin.

He commented, "I didn't expect to hear that over here."

So I had to ask, "Are you ...?"

"Yes!" he smiled, "an Inuit."

"What are you doing here?" I enquired.

He answered, "I'm on my holidays."

So now you know where Inuit folk go for a break from the snow and ice. This tale is particularly successful when my eldest daughter, Aimee Laura, follows it with the contemporary folk song 'The Last Leviathan'.

There was once a young Inuit girl called Sedna who lived in a tiny village with her father and her four brothers. She was very beautiful but had never had a boyfriend. One day, Sedna stood on the edge of the ice, peering out across the bay. In the distance she could see a stranger in a skin canoe, a kayak. This man had very pointed features and was wearing a short sealskin hooded jacket, an anorak. On the neck of the anorak there were feathers.

The stranger spotted Sedna and was instantly drawn to her beauty. He paddled towards the edge of the ice floe and flipped the canoe out of the water next to Sedna. He climbed out of the canoe, smiled as he dropped on one knee and asked Sedna to marry him. Sedna said that she would.

When she told her father and her brothers she was leaving to marry a stranger, they were shocked, but her father said, "If that is what you must do, then you must do it," because that's the way with daughters.

As her father hugged her he said, "Remember, we are your family, your people, your village. If you're unhappy, you can always return to us."

Sedna climbed into the canoe behind her lover and he paddled them out across the bay. On the shoreline her father and her brother sadly waved farewell.

In the middle of the bay, Sedna's lover seized the paddle and tossed it at the waves. Magically, the paddle transformed into a sea eagle – a great bird that soared high and dived low so that Sedna and her lover could climb on to its back. Again, the eagle soared high, bearing Sedna and her lover away to the land of the birds where they married.

But Sedna was not happy, her husband's features became more pointed and his voice higher and shriller. When he removed his anorak, she discovered those feathers were not on the hood, they were growing out of his neck. She had married the king of the birds.

After a few weeks, Sedna's father and brothers came to visit her. Seeing her unhappiness, they urged her to return with them to their village. Sedna climbed into her father's canoe, between him and her four brothers, and they paddled her towards home.

When Sedna's husband realised what had happened, he was thrown into a wild rage. He leaped into his kayak and paddled after them, but the faster he paddled the faster Sedna's father and brothers paddled.

When the husband realised he couldn't catch them, he tossed his paddle furiously at the waves and again the paddle transformed into a sea eagle, soaring high, then diving low so that the husband could ride on its back. Every time the eagle's beak touched the water's surface, the waves trebled in size.

Sedna's father's canoe started to fill with water and sink. Her brothers, terrified of drowning, realised that the only way they could survive was by tipping their own sister from the canoe and leaving her to her fate.

Sedna clung to the side of the canoe and refused to let go. In desperation, her brothers took their hunting knives and pricked her finger tips to try and make her let go. Her blood dripped into the ocean where it solidified into the shape of dolphins or porpoises – the first dolphins that ever were on this planet.

The dolphins flipped their tails and dived deep, but still Sedna clung to the canoe, which by now was half full of water. Frantically, her brothers cut the back of her hand and her blood poured into the ocean, solidifying into the shape of a walrus – that strange-tusked sea mammal.

The walrus flapped its tail and dived deep, but still Sedna clung to the side of the canoe, which by now was thee quarters full and sinking fast.

Regretfully, Sedna's father drew his hunting knife and cut her wrists. Sedna's blood pumped into the ocean, solidifying into the shape of a blue whale – the largest mammal there has ever been on this planet. The blue whale flipped its fluke, diving deep. The wash from the whale finally swept Sedna from the side of the canoe and she sank to the bottom of the ocean.

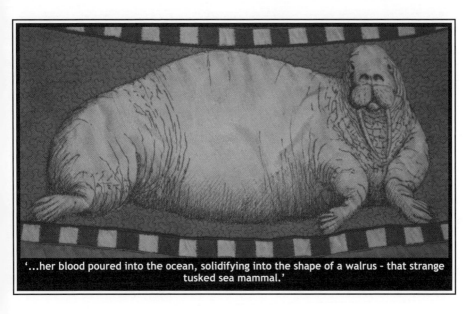

'...her blood poured into the ocean, solidifying into the shape of a walrus - that strange tusked sea mammal.'

The Inuit people will tell you that Sedna still lives at the bottom of the ocean and, from time to time, her father comes to visit her. When he visits, he combs Sedna's hair with a fish bone, for her hands are so badly damaged she is not able to comb her own hair.

When her father combs her hair, Sedna unfolds her arms and releases from her grip a seal, a walrus or a whale – just enough to supply her people with oil, meat and skin to see them through the winter months.

The Inuit people are not greedy, they only take enough to survive. Not for them the blood-red seas of the whaling ships – perhaps a lesson for us all. For that is the story of Sedna, the princess of the sea.

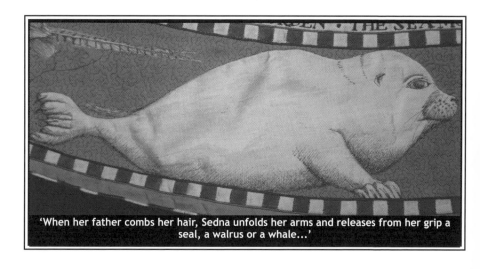

'When her father combs her hair, Sedna unfolds her arms and releases from her grip a seal, a walrus or a whale...'

THE CONEY

Although I have this as a Lake District tale, it was brought here by my dear friend and mentor, the late Duncan Williamson, one of Scotland's 'travelling people'. It is regularly told beside the River Rothay on my Grasmere storytelling walks. As Duncan once told me, "If you tell someone a story you never die."

Many years ago, before Noah was a sailor, in the vale of Grasmere, there was an animal called a coney. Now, the coney was a little bit like a squirrel; he had tiny ears and a big long bushy tail.

One day, Mr Coney was hopping along the bank of the River Rothay, which is the river that runs under the church bridge opposite the storyteller's garden. He spotted some small trout shining in the stream and wondered how he might catch one for his tea.

Who should come stomping down the river bank but old Daddy Fox.

"Ah! Mr Coney," he said. "I'll show you how to catch a fish!"

He waggled his bottom and flipped the tip of his red tail into the water. He sat patiently waiting for a bite, using his tail as a fishing line.

As soon as a fish nipped the end of his tail, he pulled it out gently, seized it in his mouth and strolled back up the fellside to feed the fish to his vixen and cubs.

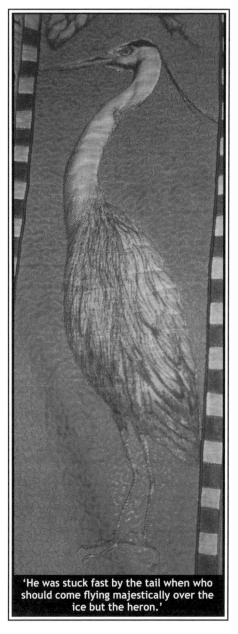

'He was stuck fast by the tail when who should come flying majestically over the ice but the heron.'

Mr Coney decided to try the same ploy. He waggled his bottom and flipped the tip of his white tail into the water. He was sat patiently waiting for a bite when who should come slithering upstream but Jack Frost. The river turned to ice, trapping Mr Coney's tail.

He was stuck fast by the tail when who should come flying majestically over the ice but the heron or, as she is known in Lakeland, the Jammy Crane.

Being a friend of Mr Coney, the heron paused to help. She seized one of Mr Coney's little ears in her beak, flapped her wings and pulled, stretching the ear. Next she seized the other ear, flapped her wings and pulled, so that Mr Coney's ears were so long that they met over the top of his head. The heron then seized both ears in her beak, flapped her wings and gave an enormous tug. There was a snapping noise as Mr Coney's tail snapped a few inches from his backside, leaving a bobbly tail like a lump of cotton wool.

Confused, Mr Coney shook his head, discovering he had long floppy ears. He looked so different with his long floppy ears and his bobbly tail that all of the other animals stopped calling him Mr Coney and started calling him 'rabbit' or 'bunny'. When, in time, he fathered his own young, they too had long ears and bobbly tails, so they were also called 'rabbits' or 'bunnies'.

So it was then and so it is now. However, if anyone ventures to a fur shop (hopefully they wouldn't, in this day and age), and if they attempted to buy a coat made of the fur of this animal, the label on the coat will not say 'rabbit fur', it will say the word 'coney' instead. This reminds everyone of the story of how Mr Coney became 'rabbit' or 'bunny', a story that a man called Charles Darwin never heard.

'There was a snapping noise as Mr Coney's tail snapped a few inches from his backside, leaving a bobbly tail like a lump of cotton wool.'

COYOTE AND THE FIRE WITCH

Throughout the 1970s and 80s, I had many good times with Scottish folk singer, 'Big' Eddie Winship - a man so tall that, when he accompanied me to school performances, the children thought he was my giant. Eddie toured a programme of songs and stories of the American Wild West, with a native American, whose name translated literally as 'Little boy who sleeps by the river where the catfish swim'. To us he was 'Catfish Jim'. Jim gave me a number of coyote stories, advising they should only be told after harvest time. He then added, "Hell, you're a friend. Tell them whenever you fancy." So I do.

The people of the tribe were freezing. They were freezing because they didn't have any fire. The only fire in the land was at the top of the mountain and was owned by the fire witch. She guarded it jealously.

The chief of the tribe sent Coyote to steal the fire. Now, Coyote was a bit like Daddy Fox, he was crafty. He took some friends with him on the mission and set off up the mountain with Chipmunk, Frog and Brown Bird. They crept up on the fire witch's tepee. Coyote seized a burning brand from the fire and set off down the mountain, pursued by the witch.

As the witch caught up with Coyote, he tossed the fire to Chipmunk. Chipmunk bravely caught the fire but it lashed across his back, burning three or four black and white scars. To this day you can still see three or four black and white stripes across the back of every chipmunk. Even baby chipmunks don't know why they're there, but we do.

Chipmunk scuttled down the mountain with the fire witch close behind.

As the witch caught up with Chipmunk, he tossed the fire to frog. However, frogs are notoriously bad at catching and the fire landed on the frog's tail, burning it clean off.

So to this day, no matter where you travel in the world, you will never find an adult frog with a tail.

Frog hopped down the mountain, with the fire witch close behind.

As she caught up with Frog, he tossed the fire to the last of his friends, Brown Bird.

Brown Bird caught the fire under one wing and flew in a circle.

'Chipmunk bravely caught the fire but it lashed across his back.'

The fire was so hot it scorched his breast, burning it bright red. Ever since that day, he has been called Robin Redbreast and he lives on both sides of the Atlantic.

Robin tossed the fire back to Coyote who bravely carried it into the middle of the village and presented it to the chief of the tribe.

He set the fire in the middle of the village and, from that day, not just that tribe but all the tribes of the world have had warmth, hot food, music and stories.

'... the fire landed on the frog's tail burning it clean off.'

THE KING'S TAILOR

THE KING'S TAILOR

*Another tale told to me by Scottish traveller,
the late Duncan Williamson.*

Many years ago, there was a little tailor, who was the finest tailor in the world. He was such a fine tailor that the king of the land called him to the palace and asked him to make all of his clothes – and I mean ALL of his clothes, from the royal robes of office to the royal boxer shorts.

The trouble was, the tailor was kept so busy making clothes for the king that, despite being the finest tailor in the world, he himself was the scruffiest, untidiest person you've ever seen. He was so scruffy and untidy, people pointed and laughed when he walked down the street.

This became an embarrassment to the king, as folk knew he was the king's tailor. So the king summoned the tailor back to the palace and forced him to look in the mirror. The king threatened the tailor that if he didn't take a day and a night to make himself some smarter clothes, he would be fired.

The tailor realised that without the money he was earning from the king, he would be much poorer.

The king realised that without the service of this little tailor, he would have to find another one, who wouldn't be as good, for after all, wasn't this little tailor the finest tailor in the world? A compromise had to be found.

The king gave the tailor a roll of the finest cloth in the land, telling him to get to work. The tailor spread the cloth on his workbench and felt it; the cloth was good. The tailor said, "Now I can make something out of that."

He set to cutting and stitching, and by the following morning he had made a jacket – not just any jacket but the finest jacket he had made in the whole of his career as a tailor. He put the jacket on and proudly looked in the mirror. Oh, he did look a dandy! As he walked down the street, everyone gazed admiringly, saying they would like a jacket just like that one.

The little tailor felt proud, proud of his craft and proud of his trade. He wore that jacket year-in and year-out. In fact, he wore it till it started to become threadbare at the elbows.

He took the jacket back to his workshop and was just about to toss it in the rubbish bin when he thought, rather than throw it away, he could recycle it. So he spread it out on his workbench and sat up all night cutting and stitching.

By the morning he had made a waistcoat – not just any waistcoat, but the finest waistcoat he had made in the whole of his career. He put the waistcoat on and proudly looked in the mirror. Oh, he did look a dandy! As he walked down the street, everyone gazed admiringly, saying they would like a waistcoat just like that one.

The little tailor felt proud, proud of his craft and proud of his trade. He wore that jacket year-in and year-out. In fact, he wore it till it started to become threadbare in the small of the back. He went back to his workshop and was just about to toss it in the rubbish bin when he thought, rather than throw it away, he could recycle it. He spread it out on his workbench and sat up all night cutting and stitching.

By the morning he had made a cloth cap – not just any cloth cap but the finest cloth cap he had made in the whole of his career. He put the cloth cap on and proudly looked in the mirror. Oh, he did look a dandy! As he walked down the street, everyone gazed admiringly, saying they would like a cloth cap just like that one.

The little tailor felt proud, proud of his craft and proud of his trade. He wore that cloth cap year-in and year-out. In fact, he wore it till it started to become threadbare across the peak. He went back to his workshop and was just about to toss it in the rubbish bin when he thought, rather than throw it away, he could recycle it. He spread it out on his workbench and sat up all night cutting and stitching.

By the morning he had made a dickie-bow tie – not just any dickie-bow tie but the finest dickie-bow tie he had made in the whole of his career. He put the dickie-bow tie on and proudly looked in the mirror. Oh, he did look a dandy! As he walked down the street, everyone gazed admiringly, saying they would like a dickie-bow tie just like that one.

'The king gave the tailor a roll of the finest cloth in the land,
telling him to get to work.'

The little tailor felt proud, proud of his craft and proud of his trade. He wore that dickie-bow tie year-in and year-out. In fact he wore it till it went threadbare and the points of the bow went floppy. He went back to his workshop and was just about to toss it in the rubbish bin when he thought rather than throw it away he could recycle it. He spread it out on his workbench and sat up all night cutting and stitching.

By the morning he had made a cloth-covered button, and sewed it on to the waistband of his trousers. He put the trousers on and proudly looked in the mirror. Oh, he did look a dandy! As he walked down the street, everyone gazed admiringly, saying they would like a cloth-covered button just like that one.

The little tailor felt proud, proud of his craft and proud of his trade. He wore that cloth-covered button year-in and year-out. In fact he wore it till it became threadbare, as the metal inside rubbed against the nap of the cloth. He went back to his workshop and was just about to snip it off and toss it in the rubbish bin when he thought rather than throw it away he could recycle it. He put it down on his workbench and he cut and he stitched, and he thought.

By the morning he'd made ... a story. He told that story to his children; they told it to their children; one of their children told it to a Scottish traveller called Duncan Williamson, and he told it to Taffy Thomas. And now that you know it, you can tell it to someone else.

THE COBBLESTONE MAKER

This was the story that gave me the power of speech as part of my recovery from a massive stroke at the age of 35. I spent much of my childhood in the company of my paternal grandfather, who lived by the moral of this tale - although he probably never heard it. He told me, "You can speak to anyone you meet in this world, from the Queen to a tramp, as long as you're polite." He could never have guessed that, as Taffy the storyteller, I would have occasion to speak both to a gentleman of the road and the Queen! I gave this story to Duncan Williamson, who thereafter always called me 'Taffy, the little cobblestone maker'.

There was a little cobblestone maker, who was the finest cobblestone maker in the world. However, he was unhappy. Whenever he did his very best work, all people did was walk on it. He wished that he could be more important, more powerful, and stronger.

So one day, he was chipping at a cobblestone, wishing he was more important, when to his amazement, he discovered that he was wearing a crown and a red cloak with white fur around the bottom. All the folk in the street bowed and knelt down, believing that he had become a king.

The cobblestone maker thought: "Great. Now, I'm important. Now, I'm powerful. Now, I'm strong. My wish has been granted. My ambition has been fulfilled."

Just then, the sun came out and all the people turned their heads to enjoy the sun.

The cobblestone maker cursed. Obviously, he thought, the sun is more important than a king. So, if I want to be more important than the sun, I must wish to be a cloud.

So he wished to be a thunder cloud, the strongest cloud of all.

There was a flash of blue light and the cobblestone maker discovered that he had become a liver-coloured cloud, floating across the sky.

All the people looked up. Seeing this dark cloud they ran for their umbrellas and raincoats.

Just to make sure that no one had missed him, the cobblestone maker sent down a flash of lightening ... followed by a crash of thunder ... followed by rain in torrents, that washed the trees from people's gardens and sent a wild river racing down through the valley.

The cobblestone maker thought, "Great. Now, I'm important. Now,

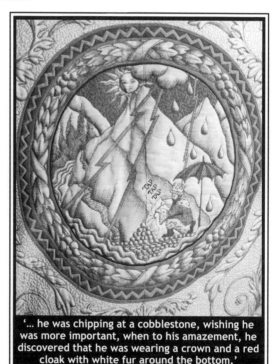

'... he was chipping at a cobblestone, wishing he was more important, when to his amazement, he discovered that he was wearing a crown and a red cloak with white fur around the bottom.'

I'm powerful. Now, I'm strong. My wish has been granted. My ambition has been fulfilled."

The river crashed into a granite mountain, splitting into two streams, one on each side of the mountain. Again the cobblestone maker cursed. A mountain is more important than a flooded river, he thought. So, if I want to be more important than that, I must wish to be a granite mountain.

As he made his wish, there was a flash of blue light, and the cobblestone maker became a granite mountain, standing four-square at the head of the valley.

There he stayed as the days became weeks, the weeks became months and the months became years.

One morning, he woke with a tickling, itching on his back. He looked around and there, on the back of the mountain, chipping away patiently, was ... a little cobblestone maker.

Finally, the little cobblestone maker realised that he *was* important: he didn't need to be a king, a cloud or even a mountain, because people rely on people, just like him, to give them the things they need.

And so the one who chips away at the rocks is just as important as the one who builds the roads. And the one who cleans the hospitals is just as important as the one who performs the operations. And the storyteller is just as important as the police officer, the teacher or the politician – but no more so.

THE HUNCHBACK AND THE SWAN

This is one of my favourite stories. Again, it was gifted to me by Duncan Williamson on many occasions. I have told this story to friends by Grasmere lake only to notice two resident mute swans swimming towards us to listen. Now that's magic!

On the fellside near the lake in Grasmere is a little thatch cottage, and many years ago in that cottage lived a hunchback – an old man with a hump on his back, an old man so ugly that the people in the village would have nothing to do with him. Furthermore, the hunchback was completely mute. His only friends were the animals of the forest. So sometimes, when he went collecting sticks, he was followed by a line of animals – the weasel, the rabbit, the badger, the fox and, flying overhead, the robin and the wren. The hunchback also had one very special friend – a swan who lived down on the lake. He so loved that swan that he called her his 'lady of the lake'. Sometimes the swan waddled after him and he'd half turn and stroke her beautiful curved neck.

Now, one winter the hunchback disappeared. Was he alive or was he dead? The people in the village didn't care, but the animals cared because they weren't getting their breadcrumbs and their saucers of milk. So the animals went to find out.

Off went the line of animals – the weasel, the rabbit, the badger, the fox and, flying over head, the robin and the wren – off up the lane towards the hunchback's cottage. They made a circle around the cottage as the robin fluttered up to the window to peep in. The hunchback was lying on the bed completely still and the robin whispered back to the other animals, "I think he may be dead!"

Just then, the robin tapped his little yellow beak three times on the window and the flicker of a smile spread across the hunchback's face. Excited, the robin reported back, "No, he's still alive but he's desperately sick."

The animals knew they needed help. They needed the help of the wisest of birds, the wise old Owl, or to give it its Lakeland name, the hulet.

The robin flew off to the wood to where the hulet was perched on a branch. Settling next to the owl, the robin reported the sickness of the hunchback.

The hulet advised the robin that if the hunchback got a visit from his special friend, his lady of the lake, it may cure him.

Thanking the hulet, the robin flew off to the lake to where the swan was settled in her nest. Landing next to the swan, he told her of the hunchback's sickness, adding the owl's advice that she might be able to save him.

The swan climbed from the nest and swam to the other bank. Then she started to waddle up the path toward the hunchback's cottage. So, there was the swan followed by the line of animals – the weasel, the rabbit, the badger, the fox and, flying over head, the robin and the wren.

They formed a circle around the cottage – a magic circle. As the swan waddled up to the back door and pushed it open with her yellow bill, the wren fluttered up to the window to peep in. The hunchback was lying on a white sheet. His face was as white as the sheet he was lying on and he was completely motionless.

The wren whispered to the others, "It may be too late," then, "No, wait a minute, my lady is waddling over to the bed."

The swan tapped her yellow bill on the hunchback's forehead three times and he started to smile. Excited, the wren reported, "We're in time, he's still alive!"

'The hunchback also had one very special friend - a swan who lived down on the lake'

Just then, the swan tore some of the feathers from her left wing and jabbed them through the skin of the hunchback's left arm, where they remained. Then, the swan tore some of the feathers from her right wing and jabbed them through the skin of the hunchback's right arm, where again they stayed.

On hearing this, the circle of animals became very agitated and asked the wren, "What's happening now?"

The wren reported that the hunchback had rolled over and the swan had torn some feathers from her back and jabbed them through the skin of his back.

Inside the cottage, the swan then started to stroke the hunchback's hump with her yellow bill and his back flattened out. Then, stroking the hunchback's neck with her bill, his neck became long and curved.

It had gone magically quiet and the animals wondered what was happening.

After some magical time, the back door of the cottage opened and, to the animals' amazement, out waddled not one but two swans. The swans waddled down to the lake, slid into the water and swam off side by side.

They say our friend the hunchback will be with his lady of the lake for ever now, because swans, like most water foul, only mate once in their lifetime, and they mate for life! However, strangely, since that day, most of the swans in the Lake District are mute ... just like the hunchback in our story.

COAT TAILS

This story was brought to Britain by Israeli storyteller, Sharon Aviv. However, two friends, Irish-American storyteller, Patrick Ryan, and a teenage lass from Keighley, both told me this tale as a 50th birthday present, believing it had a home with a man with a coat. It was my choice for the first story I would tell in the new 21st century at 00:05 for friends by the bonfire in Allendale, Northumberland.

There was once a man who had a coat with beautiful pictures on it and, wherever he went, he was made welcome.

But at the same time, there was a woman who was plain; in fact, from some angles you might even say she was ugly. When she went to the same places as the man, doors were shut, lights went out and people pretended they weren't at home.

The woman went to the man and said, "My name is Truth, and no matter where I go, people try to avoid me."

She asked the man why he was always welcome and she wasn't.

The man said, "My name is Story," and explained that there was always more hospitality offered to him than he could handle.

He suggested that the woman hide under his coat and travel with him.

And so it has been, ever since that day, that whenever you hear a good story, very close to it you will find Truth – sometimes walking hand in hand and sometimes clinging to its coat tails.

'There was once a man who had a coat with beautiful pictures on it and, wherever he went, he was made welcome'

THE STORYTELLER'S GARDEN

S ince 2000, Taffy Thomas has been the Director and Storyteller in Residence at the Storyteller's Garden, located at the heart of the village of Grasmere in England's Lake District.

From the Storyteller's Garden, Taffy runs storytelling training courses and has helped to mentor a number of emerging storytellers. Along with his wife, Chrissy, Taffy also organises a programme of seasonal events held in this unique and original open-air venue, which are, they say, 'for the young and for the young at heart'. All year round, the garden – which is leased from the National Trust – attracts a rich mixture of visitors and locals who are always made very welcome. Provided Taffy is not away performing on tour, he is happy to respond to requests to meet people. Those who call, seldom leave without being told a story or asked a riddle.

As part of its work since 1995, the Storyteller's Garden also hosts a monthly storytelling club on the first Tuesday of every month at the Watermill Inn in Ings, near Kendal.

You can find out more by visiting Taffy's website at *www.taffythomas.co.uk*.

THE NATION'S FIRST LAUREATE FOR STORYTELLING

In January 2010, during the tenth National Storytelling Week, Taffy Thomas, MBE, officially accepted the honorary position of first Laureate for Storytelling, a two-year post backed by Liverpool poet, Brian Patten, and former Children's Laureate Michael Rosen.

Taffy pledged, "I will do all within my power to promote the art and to encourage the passing on of both repertoire and skills. I will endeavour to lay a firm foundation for future storytelling laureates and believe this is an exciting new development for storytelling, and I am delighted and honoured to be involved at the start of a new chapter in the life of our art."

Taffy was given seven special gifts to carry with him while undertaking official engagements across the UK: a 1kg bag of dried beans, a simple compass, a packet of Love Hearts, a clear glass bottle, a tall white candle, a silver lucky charm bracelet and a whistle.

The official patrons and 'guardians of the story' include: the Liverpool poet Brian Patten; Michael Rosen – poet, broadcaster and former Children's

Laureate; storyteller Peter Chand; Simon Thirsk, Chairman of Bloodaxe Books; Del Reid, National Director of Storytelling Week; and Patsy Heap, Director of Children's Services and Libraries in Birmingham.

Endorsing the Laureateship, Brian Patten said: "Taffy will make a great ambassador for storytelling." Michael Rosen added: "I'm so pleased for Taffy. Anything that helps support the oral tradition of storytelling gets my vote."

The honorary position is awarded and organised by the Smethwick-based independent production company, 'kindandgenerous', and is the initiative of poet and writer, Adrian Johnson. "Stories inspire and encourage us at critical moments in our lives," said Adrian, "and with the brilliant success of the Poet Laureate and other regional projects the time seemed right to honour the oral tradition of storytelling and those that tell them."

USEFUL WEBSITES:

www.taffythomas.co.uk   To engage the services of storyteller, Taffy Thomas, with the Tale Coat, or to purchase Taffy's CDs.

www.paddykillerart.co.uk   For more information on the work of Paddy Killer.

TAFFY'S COAT TALES – ADDITIONAL CREDITS:

Editor:	Helen Watts
Sub-Editor:	Sarah Sodhi
Designer:	Chris Sweeney
Photography:	Pieter Koster, Louise Hemsley, and Steven Barber Photography (www.stevenbarber.com).

OTHER PUBLICATIONS BY TAFFY THOMAS MBE

BOOKS

Cumbrian Folk Tales (97807524071273); Midwinter Folk Tales (9780750955881) and First World War Folk Tales (9780750958325, co-written with Helen Watts) all published by The History Press.

Stories from the Storyteller's Garden (Tales in Trust).

Tales and Trails from the Storyteller's Garden, Grasmere (Tales in Trust).

Three Golden Apples (Tales in Trust).

Farmer Merryweather's Cow (Tales in Trust).

The Linking of the Chain: Legends of the North (Tales in Trust).

Telling Tales: Storytelling as Emotional Literacy by Taffy Thomas and Steve Killick (Educational Printing Services, 9781905637287).

CDS

All available from Tales in Trust:

Tales in Trust (TTCD04).

Take these Chains from My Heart (TTCD06).

Favourite Tales from the Tale Coat (TTCD08).

Stories from the Storyteller's Garden (TTCD09).

Ghosts (TTCD10).

Fairy Gold (TTCD11).

Legends of the North (TTCD12).

The Little Cobblestone Maker (TTCD13).

Tales for the Young and the Young at Heart (TTCD14).

Tell Someone a Story for Christmas (Lyngham House Music, Lyng 218CD).

MULTIMEDIA

The Gingerbread Man compiled by Pie Corbett (Scholastic, 9781407100647). Children's book and CD for ages 4 to 7. Accompanying Storyteller teacher pack (9781407100678).

Dragonory compiled by Pie Corbett (Scholastic Storyteller series, 9781407100654). Children's book and CD for ages 7 to 9. Accompanying Storyteller teacher pack (9781407100685).

The Boy and the Tiger compiled by Pie Corbett (Scholastic Storyteller series, 9781407100661). Children's book and CD for ages 9 to 11. Accompanying Storyteller teacher pack (9781407100692).

For details of all Tales in Trust publications, visit www.taffythomas.co.uk email info@taffythomas.co.uk or write to: Tales in Trust, The Storyteller's House, Oak Bank, Rydal Road, Ambleside, Cumbria LA22 9BA, UK.